GOLDEN BOOKS & DESIGN,™ A GOLDEN BOOK,® and
the distinctive gold spine are trademarks of Western Publishing Company, Inc.

A GOLDEN BOOK®
Western Publishing Company, Inc.
Racine, Wisconsin 53404

Find and circle the cowboy words.
Look across and down.

WORD LIST

BANDANNA   GLOVES

BADGE   HAT

BELT   HORSE

BOOTS   SPURS

```
G  L  O  L  A  V  T  K  H
R  B  A  N  D  A  N  N  A
I  A  P  B  E  M  U  I  T
L  D  H  O  R  S  E  D  H
S  G  C  O  T  P  B  U  C
B  E  L  T  R  U  D  O  F
O  K  Y  S  A  R  V  E  A
G  L  O  V  E  S  I  B  H
```

Draw Hamm. Use the top picture as a guide.

How many times can you find the word TOYS in this puzzle?

T O Y S Y O T
O T S Y O T O
Y O T O Y S Y
S Y O T O Y S
Y Y O T O S Y
O T S O Y S O
T O Y S Y O T

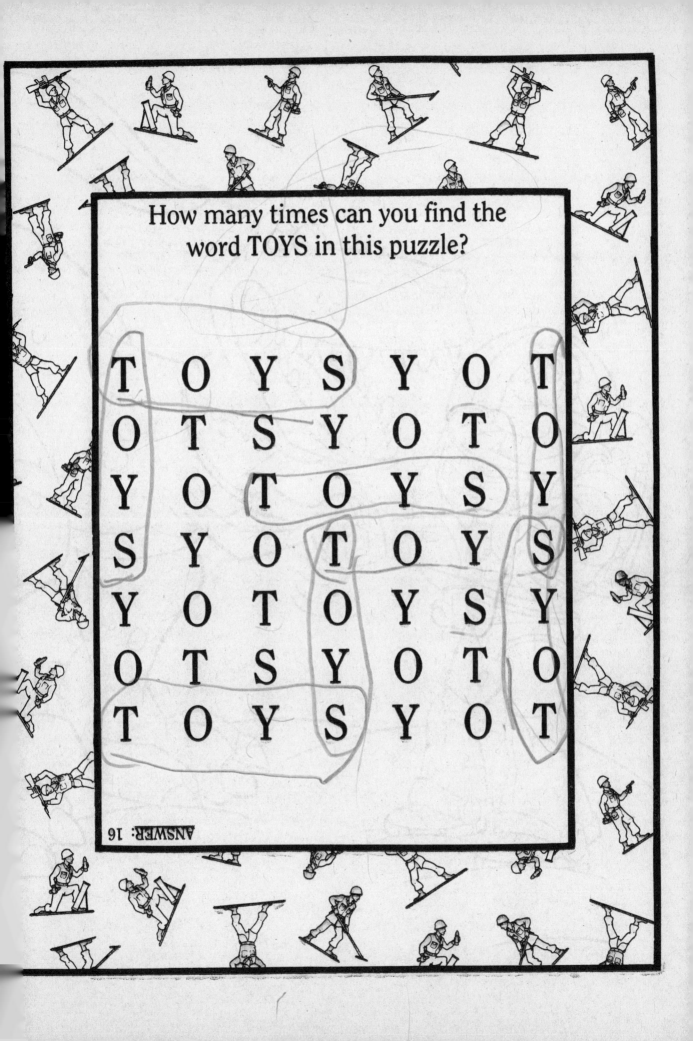

Can you find the real Buzz Lightyear?
[Hint: He's the only one that is different!]

Draw a picture of your favorite toy.

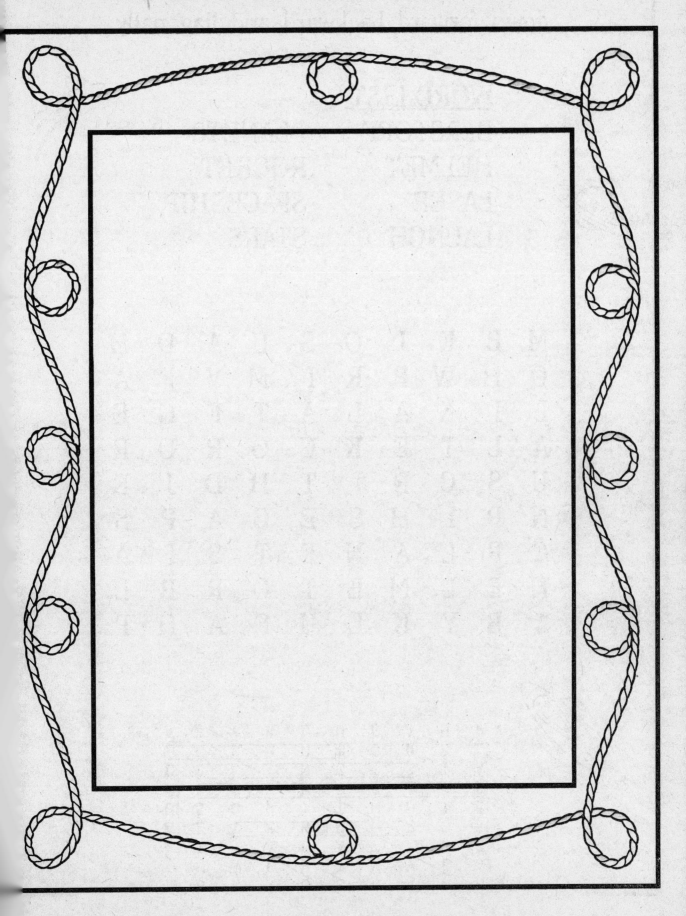

Find and circle the space words. Look up,
down, forward, backward, and diagonally.

WORD LIST

BLASTOFF	PLANETS
HELMET	ROCKET
LASER	SPACESHIP
LAUNCH	STARS

```
M  B  E  J  O  S  U  A  D  H
O  H  W  P  R  I  M  V  F  A
L  I  N  A  L  A  T  F  G  E
A  L  T  E  K  C  O  R  O  R
U  S  C  R  I  T  H  D  J  E
N  P  I  H  S  E  C  A  P  S
C  P  L  A  N  E  T  S  I  A
H  E  L  M  E  T  O  R  B  L
A  B  Y  K  L  U  F  A  H  P
```

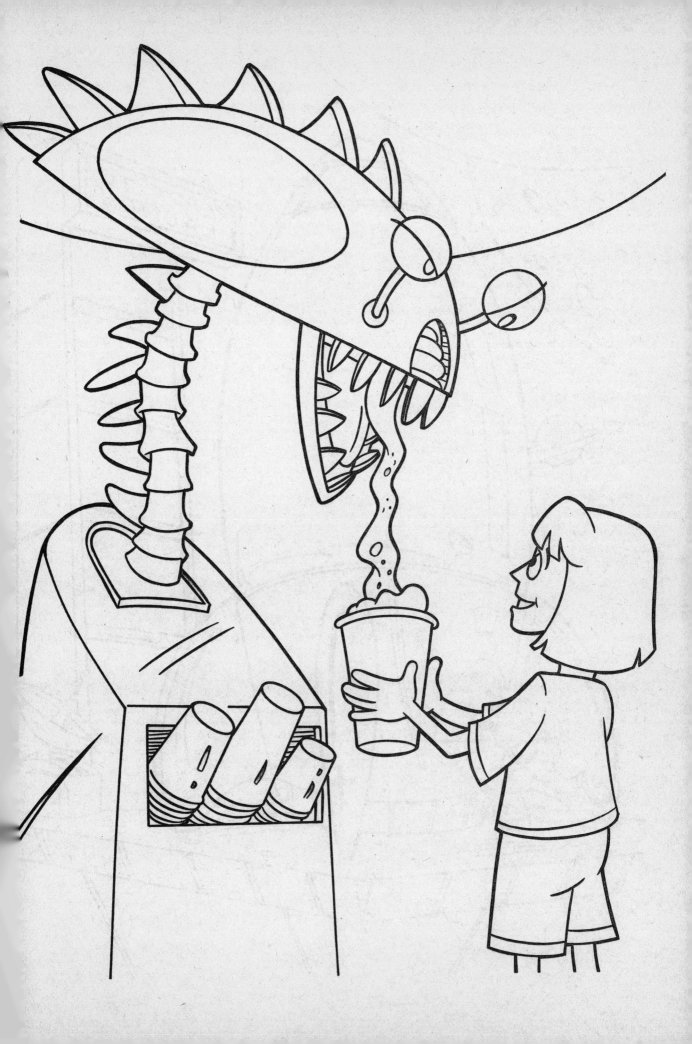

Design your own spaceship.

POSSIBLE ANSWERS: ARE, ART, AT, ATE, BAG, BAT, BATH, BAY, BEAR, BET, BIG, BIT, BRIGHT, BUG, BUT, BUY, EAR, EARLY, EAT, GET, GRAB, GREAT, GUT, HAIL, HAT, HAY, HEAL, HEAR, HEAT, HER, HUG, IT, LAUGH, LAY, LEG, LET, LIGHT, LIT, RAIL, RAT, RAY, REAL, RUG, TABLE, TAIL, TAR, TEA, TEAR, TRAY, TUB, TUG, YEAR, YET, ZEBRA

_____   _____   _____

_____   _____   _____

_____   _____   _____

_____   _____   _____

_____   _____   _____

_____   _____   _____

How many words can you make from the
letters in BUZZ LIGHTYEAR?

DOT GAME
(A GAME FOR TWO OR MORE PLAYERS)

Take turns drawing a straight line between any two dots to make a square. When you make a square, put your initials in it and take another turn. Count 1 point for empty squares, and 2 points for squares with Woody or Buzz. When all the dots have been connected, the player with the most points wins.

PLAY THE DOT GAME AGAIN!

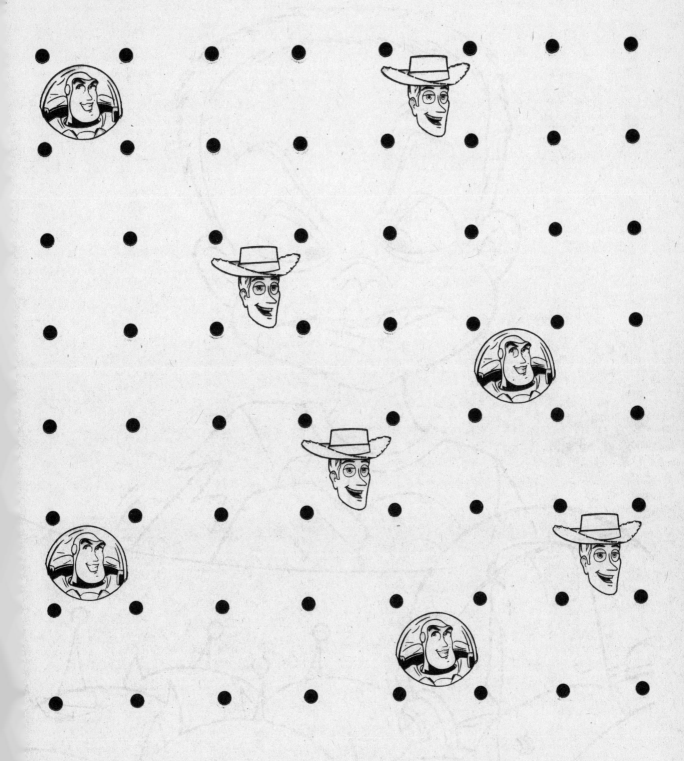

Look carefully at
the picture on
these two pages.
Then turn the page.

How many
differences
can you find?

Draw your own mutant toy.

Cut around the door sign and on the dotted line. Color both sides of the sign. Hang the sign on the doorknob to your room.

SHERIFF'S OFFICE

ANDY

SPACE HEADQUARTERS

Draw your best friend.

LIGHTYEAR

MEMORY CARD GAME
(A GAME FOR TWO PLAYERS)

Tear out the next two pages. Carefully cut out the playing cards along the dotted lines. Mix them up and arrange them in rows of four, number side down. The first player turns over two cards. If the numbers on the cards match, the player sets them aside and takes another turn. If the numbers do not match, the cards are replaced facedown and the next player takes a turn. Play continues until all of the cards have been matched. The player with the most pairs wins!

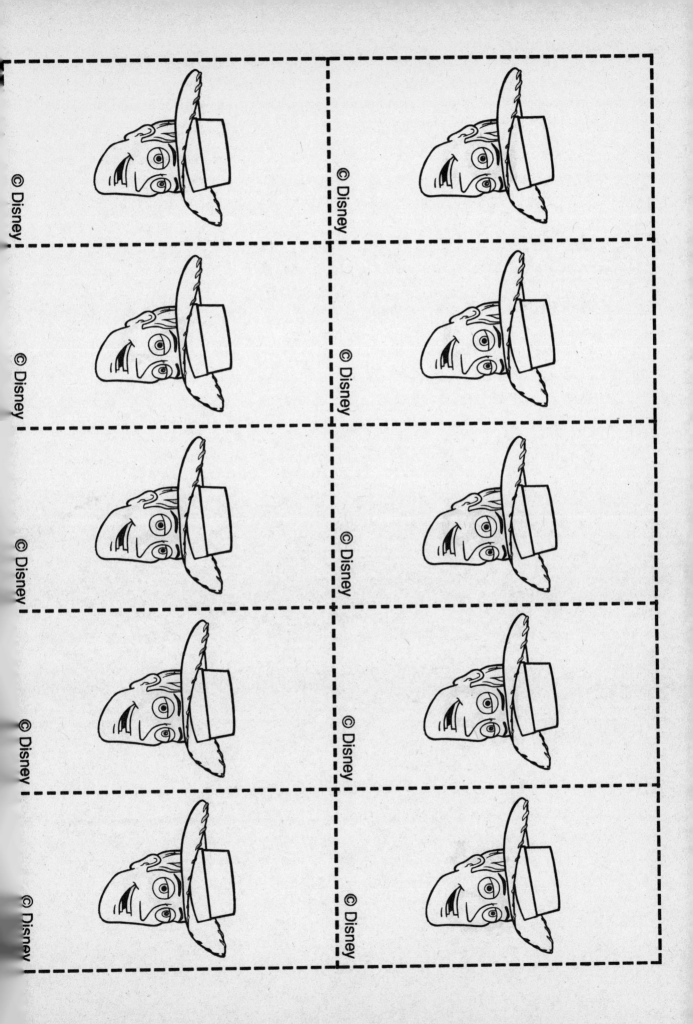

1

2

3

4

5

6

7

8

9

10

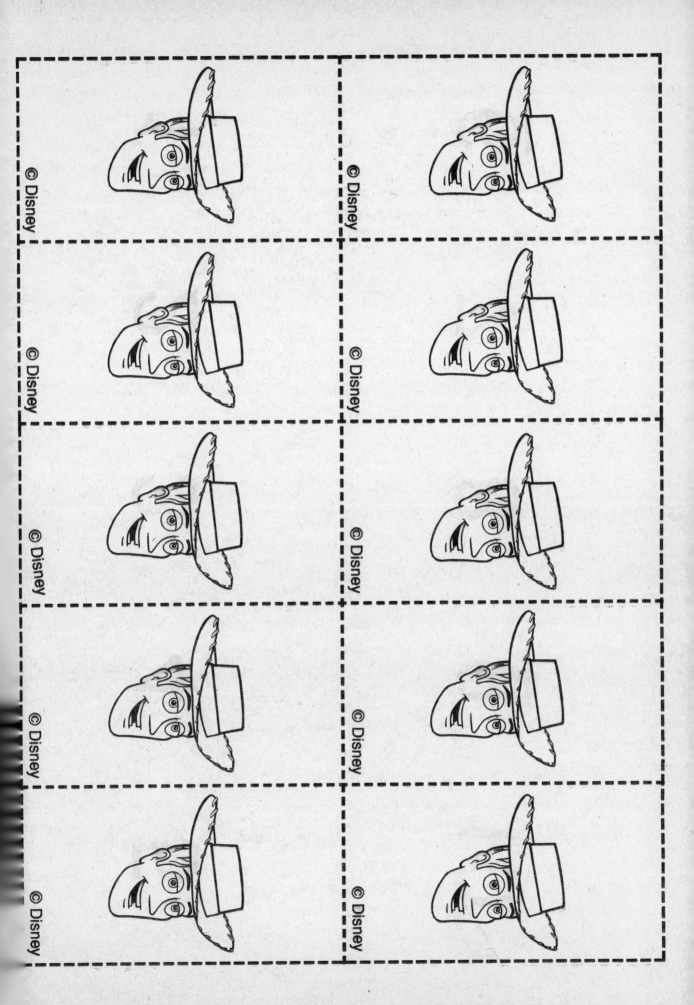

1

2

3

4

5

6

7

8

9

10

Woody and Buzz become best buddies.
Unscramble these words to learn what best
buddies do together or for one another.

ARCE   _____

LEHP   _____

GLUHA   _____

RALEN   _____

YALP   _____

SARHE   _____

KROW   _____

Help Woody and Buzz find their way back to Andy.

Tear out the next two mini-poster pages.
Color the pictures and hang them in your room.